THAT CAT
is the laziest cat in the world

FOR
DOM & ALEX BURFORD
JACKSON & JOSHUA HEATH

For
Madeline
Best
J-F

7/2/17

J-F BURFORD   IAN HEATH

All he does is sleep

he sleeps in the morning

he sleeps in the Afternoon

He sleeps at night.....

...ALL HE DOES IS SLEEP

That cat is the laziest cat in the world

Original Idea © J-F Burford 2016
Research and Text © J-F Burford © Ian Heath 2016
All illustrations and designs © Ian Heath © J-F Burford 2016

First Edition 2016

Printed By Blissetts of London

ISBN Number: 978-1-905912-46-9
A catalogue record or this book is available from the British Library.

First published in the United Kingdom, 2016
By That Lazy Cat Ltd 4 High Park Road London TW9 4BH

For news and other titles visit: www.thatlazycat.co.uk
To get in touch email: Info@thatlazycat.co.uk